Shadowball on the Hill

Earl Wyatt II

spike.fish

Shadowball on the Hill

Earl Wyatt II

Published by:
Spike.fish
700 Pennsylvania Ave SE
Washington, DC 20003

Cover Design: Earl Wyatt II

ISBN-13: 979-8-218-67425-0

Printed in USA

Dedications

To Dad, Mom, Eboni and Tayler for the foundation

To KJH for the motivation

Table of Contents

PROLOGUE

Pittsburgh
Thursday, April 28, 1932
11:30pm

"Daaaad, I promise... I'll help mom with the kids tomorrow, no excuses. We've still got customers and I'm making really good tips here. Please let me stay..."

Marie paused, knowing her father would surrender to her pitch-perfect begging. Of course, he hated the begging but loved that she had the job and a solid work ethic.

"Thanks Dad... I just have to finish closing up here. I'll be home before you know it."

She paused once more... And this time she smiled.

"Love you too!"

She hung up.

Nine days into her twenty-first year, Marie Franks finally felt like an adult. Her father even said so, though not in so many words. But conceding on a curfew was inconceivable in the past.

But why not? She was making her own money away from the family daycare. In fact, she'd already paid 15 dollars towards the 50 dollar lemon yellow dress they were holding for her at Sam Reznik & Sons. She didn't know much about finance, but according to her calculations, spending 50 dollars to look like a million dollars was a reasonably savvy investment.

Two more weeks' worth of shifts and she would turn heads, guaranteed.

Oh, that dress...

Marie checked her hair in the mirror by the bar, then glanced down to make sure her slip wasn't visible. She slid on her uniform's white gloves, and carefully picked up the service tray full of drinks, which was waiting for her at the end of the bar.

Elegantly, Marie glided into the main dining room of the Crawford Grill. With each step, her modest black heels landed in precise alignment just as Mistress Holden had trained her at the nearby Charm School for Colored Girls. She was so smooth, the drinks and ice cubes never moved.

The Grill — a regular haunt of connected negroes in the Hill District — was always saturated with smoke, the latest jazz, and melanin in its most uppity form.

Earlier tonight was no different. But now... after 11 pm, the good folks who didn't allow the government to *prohibit* them from a stiff drink after a long day of work, had gone home. Now The Grill was simply a speakeasy, with one remaining table full of well-dressed clientele.

Marie, still in the "making a good first impression" phase of her employment, doubted she'd ever get used to the clientele. Some were famous. Some were infamous. But all, as her father would say, were colored *and* colorful.

Humming along to the melody of Duke Ellington's *Mood Indigo* as it blared through the speakers, she served drinks to the remaining patrons; six men in dark suits seated together with their fedoras on the adjacent tables.

Having just heard their raucous laughter while at the bar, she couldn't help but notice they'd grown silent as she neared the table. (Exactly like the mischievous boys at her mother's daycare.)

She thought, "Do the naughty boys ever grow up?"

"I got two vodka martinis up, scotch neat, and bourbon rocks," Marie announced.

John L. Clarke, a tall black man in his early thirties, tapped his pen on a closed steno pad, then snapped back from wherever his mind was while reaching for his bourbon.

A once athletic black man now in his late thirties, Edwin "Teddy" Fletcher Horne, Jr., was the only man who had placed his hat on the table in front of him, and was clearly holding court among the other suits.

Lamar "Brick" Torrence, a short but muscular black man in his early thirties, rose from his seat to gently instruct Marie to leave the tray. With kind eye contact, Brick acknowledged Marie's hard work, and shared an encouraging, "Doing great Shorty... Keep it up." He squeezed a small fold of money into her gloved hand.

Marie responded with a modest smile, nodded to express her gratitude, then returned to her original task of cleaning the bar. Once behind the bar, she opened her hand and saw that she could buy two dresses with Brick's tip.

Oh, that dress...

Back at the table, John continued the conversation, "I mean what did he say after that? And Teddy, can I please go on the record now?"

Teddy's eyes glimmered with mischief as he asserted, "Notebook stays closed... Cumberland Posey, Mr. Black high society himself, stood there slack-jawed. He just learned that every drop of talent from his precious Homestead Grays had gone to his archenemy, Gus Greenlee. What could he say?"

John mused, "Well, Posey could have said Gus overpaid to the tune of a few thousand dollars..."

Teddy leaned forward and counted with his fingers for emphasis as he rattled off names with the flourish of a radio announcer: "Satchel Paige, the human flamethrower... James "Cool Papa" Bell, a man I've personally seen circle the bases in 13 seconds... The black Babe Ruth himself... Josh Gibson? Listen to me... If Posey thinks Gus overpaid, he wasn't meant to own a team full of legends in their prime."

The other gents at the table laughed and clapped. Brick smiled, raised his scotch, a toast to Gus. All raised their glasses to join him in the spontaneous tribute.

John shook his head, "That's a bad dude..."

The room paused as Teddy, with a swift and unexpected move, placed a gun on the table. "Why, John? What exactly have you heard?

The dining room, warmed by both a woodburning stove and Duke Ellington on the speakers, went still, silent, cold. John could actually hear beads of sweat form on his forehead and the back of his neck.

John stammered, searching Teddy's face for the slightest micro-expression to give him any assurances of mercy... or even humanity. The tension built until...

Teddy exploded in laughter. "You should have seen your face! I should make you pay for those watered-down bourbons you're drinking. Brick! Check his pants for wetness." Brick, still laughing, shook his head. "Nah, T, I don't think I will."

Although Marie was out of earshot of whatever was

said, she answered her own question. The naughty boys never do grow up.

Once the bar was cleaned and restocked, Marie approached Teddy and Brick, concealing her joy at the generous tip, "Sirs, will you need anything else tonight?"

Teddy glanced at his watch and said, "No, we should be good for the rest of the night. Thanks for everything, Janet."

Marie looked slightly puzzled. "Sir...?"

Brick interjected, "T, Janet is the other new server... This is Marie... You know, Diahann and Marion Frank's little girl? One of Lena's girlfriends."

Teddy recollected and addressed Marie warmly, "Marie! That's right... Forgive me, it's been a long day and a late night... Wait... You're off tomorrow, right?"

Marie nodded, "I'll be helping my mother with her daycare the next few days. But I'm back on Monday."

Teddy raised his glass again and said, "Tell your folks I said hello." Looking at Brick he offered, "That man made me a lot of money back in the day."

Marie responded, "I will. And please give my best to Lena." Teddy smiled and said he would.

As Marie walked toward the door, Teddy called after her, "You know what, Marie? Go 'head and lock the door behind you... All our cars are actually parked out back."

"Yes sir."

Marie turned off the Crawford Grill's sign. The bar was officially closed. She stepped outside, thinking about how she would get to Reznik's during business hours. Surely Mom would let her take a lunch break, and the store wasn't too far to walk... And if the dress didn't need to be hemmed, she might be able to wear it to Opening Day on Sunday!

Oh that dress!

It's possible she hadn't heard the car pull up behind her as she locked the front door with the rusted key they gave the newest employees. (A form of hazing Gus endorsed.) It was a bit cumbersome to get it into the lock. She dropped the key loosely into her purse.

If she didn't hear the car pull up, she definitely wasn't aware that the driver shut off the car's headlights while trailing her halfway down the empty sidewalk.

A voice from the car window said charmingly, and with a slight drawl, "Now what's a pretty little thing like you doing out here alone? That just ain't right." Marie pretended to hear nothing and stepped quicker.

In a thicker drawl, a second voice said, "Now where I'm from, we'd never let that happen."

Marie turned around, clearly uncomfortable, and responded politely, "That's okay. Thank you kindly."

She glanced down the street, and thoughts of a yellow dress and accessories were suddenly replaced by, "Can I get to the end of the block if I have to run?"

But she decided against it and quickly pivoted back toward the Grill. Having kicked off her heels, she grabbed them with shaking hands, then ran in her stocking feet over the scattered pebbles and broken glass. Where were the keys she had just dropped in her purse?

She heard the tires squeal as the car was thrown in reverse with what could only be described as an aggressive amount of gas.

She found the key!

She reached the door to the Grill. She fumbled to get the key into the lock, the rust making it harder than before, while adrenaline and fearful tears blurred her vision. The light above the door was dark.

The car door opened.

"No no no no no you don't," she heard the voice, now outside the car. An oil-stained laborer's glove covered her mouth and the man snatched her as she expressed a muffled shriek.

In her struggle, Marie kicked the door, making a sound which echoed along the empty street. Car doors slammed, tires squealed, and the car sped off into the otherwise placid night.

Mercilessly, the light above the sign flickered on.

Inside the Grill, Teddy heard the commotion. He opened the door and looked around to only see taillights in the distance. He frowned.

He could have sworn he heard something, but after a moment of searching, he shrugged and returned to the table

"Brick, I guess I was wrong... There's nothing out there. Start the car, I'll be right there."

He closed the door. He locked it.

And with the flip of a switch the light above the Crawford Grill sign went dark once again.

Chapter 1

Friday, April 29, 1932
Noon.

"He's no batter!"

Lil Smitty loved how support for him as a pitcher often came in the form of insults from his teammates directed at his opponents.

The school yard games held at Herron Hill Junior High have only been open to spectators for about a year... But as far as traditions go, the Hill District already adopted it.

Weather-permitting, Fridays during spring meant students had half-days in the classroom. They divided into teams, wore their homemade jerseys, volunteers took turns umpiring, and neighbors were given a reason to gather in bleachers and lawn chairs to cheer.

Ice cream was often sold in the parking lot but was free for the kids on the winning team.

So while it wasn't Yankee Stadium, the passion for the game by players and fans alike distracted from the aged equipment and unkempt field.

Calvin "Lil Smitty" Smith II, already a local favorite at 14, made a name for himself with his fastball... And its lack of control. It wasn't always clear if the batters he faced were swinging offensively to hit the ball, or defensively to protect their vital organs.

Either way, it seemed they never had enough time to swing. So when he was on the mound, the crowd heard the ball hit the worn leather in the catcher's mitt more often than the crack of a bat.

9th inning
Score 1-0
2 outs

Smitty was already beginning to taste the vanilla ice cream.

The young pitcher drew back, then hurled his next pitch... No surprise, a wild fastball. This time though, it flew through the air at an upward angle and connected with the bill of the batter's soft cap.

"Batter hit! Take first base young man."

Smitty's raspy reply, "C'mon ump! It didn't hit him… It hit his hat!"

Across the street, a city bus stopped. When it pulled away, Michael, a black man in his mid-thirties, fresh soot and 15 years of hard labor on his face, used a cane to hurriedly limp across the street toward the game.

Smitty was still pleading his case as Michael walked past the ice cream vendor, hobbled through uneven grass, and found a hidden place in the bleachers to lean.

Mac, a short beanpole of an 11-year-old, the number 20 drawn on the back of his jersey, moved to take practice swings in the on-deck circle as a formality.

He wasn't expecting to get an at-bat, and Smitty was certain to get his third out with the last guy. But with a hit batter Mac's at-bat was inevitable. Well whenever Smitty was able to accept the rules of the game, that is.

"Next batter!" the ump declared.

Mac stretched his neck to look around at the crowd. Michael ducked. Then Mac left the on-deck circle and stepped past cheering teammates to the plate. Ultra focused, he knocked the dirt off of his shoes, spit, then straightened his hat the way he'd seen real ballplayers do. He set up in the right-handed batter's box and rested the bat on his shoulders.

Michael smiled. Happy not to miss this.

Smitty did a quick lap around the pitcher's mound and talked to his teammates, loud enough for everyone to hear, "It's their lil catcher. I've struck him out a bunch of times... We'll be eating ice cream in no time."

Michael rolled his eyes... But thought to himself, "Not so fast... C'mon buddy."

Mac said nothing, but looked at the tying run on first base. He went through his batter's box ritual again. Swinging the bat around to loosen his wrists but trying to synchronize the tightening of his grip to peak when he made contact.

The first pitch was a right–to–left slider in the dirt away from Mac. He swung and missed.

"Strike one!"

"Hahaha... Told ya'll he ain't got it in him. Easy out," Smitty said, taking another lap around the pitcher's mound for dramatic effect.

Mac's eyes deepened; his focus clear. He rested the bat on his shoulder before taking a few more practice swings.

Michael, still hidden in the crowd, clenched his fists and thought, "Alright buddy watch the next one... He's trying to get you on junk... Make him earn it."

The second pitch came... Mac didn't swing. During the pitch, the runner on first ran to steal second base.

"Strike two!"

The runner slid safely into second. Barely beating the catcher's attempt to throw him out, the shortstop covering the bag missed the catch. The errant ball went into shallow centerfield. The runner got up off the dirt and ran for his life to successfully slide safely into third.

With the tying run on third base, the crowd of school kids cheered loudly, some yelling, "Strike him out!" while others yelled, "Take your time!"

Mac tightened his grip, then stopped, held up his hand, and asked for a quick time-out. The umpire allowed him a second to collect himself.

Meanwhile, Michael's body was beginning to fail him. He knew he shouldn't have left his back brace at work. He gripped his cane and thought, "Just breathe buddy... You can do it, Mac."

Mac looked around at the crowd. When his eyes moved toward Michael's direction, Michael ducked, which wasn't easy to do quickly. Mac didn't see him... Frowned a little to himself... Then stepped back in the batter's box. He gripped the bat until his ebony knuckles turned nearly white.

Smitty glanced at third base then back to home plate, and at a volume intended only for Mac he said, "Never you mind about that boy over there on third base! Ya see he ain't crossing that plate you're standing on... Cause I'mma strike you out."

Mac's internal reply, "Whatever man... Just put it in here... If you can."

The wind up... The pitch... A loud crack of the bat. A high fly ball to center field... The runner on third slowly trotted toward home plate. The center fielder also trotted back toward the fence, first slowly then quicker... And caught the ball, ending the game. Mac, deflated, returned to the dugout.

Michael frowned with tight lips, "Shake it off buddy... You'll get 'em next time. There's always tomorrow."

Racing the crowd away from the sandlot, Michael limped over to his return bus stop. He made it in time to climb into the bus, which had just arrived.

A crowd of kids surrounded the young pitcher, calling out, "SMITTY! SMITTY!"

Mac walked back to the dugout, grabbed his glove, then quickly left the sandlot. He had no interest in sticking around.

Who really *needs* ice cream anyway?

Chapter 2

On the third floor of the Pittsburgh Courier building, John, steno pad open, sat in his boss's office for hours.

Now in his mid-fifties, Robert Vann had been the publisher of the Courier for years, but was less a fan of journalism than the influence it allowed him to wield in Pittsburgh.

Both were frustrated at how their conversation had, so far, gone in circles.

Robert started again, "...Alright give me your excuse from the beginning. I promise I'll try harder to listen this time..."

John, playing along, "He's actually a Republican."

"That part, I know."

"And you want me to help YOU talk him into backing a Democrat."

"Uhhhh."

"What's wrong?"

"I don't want you to help me, as much as I..."

"Want me to do it for you."

"Yeah. And he's not just any Democrat. He's Roosevelt. W.E.B. DuBois himself says this in our best interest. That's gospel as far as I'm concerned."

"And it has to be me, because he's a bootlegger who runs the numbers racket and goes nowhere without two gun-wielding suits at all times."

Robert straightened the lapel on his jacket to preen, then smiled in a predictably pretentious way.

"Well I *am* on the deacon board."

Not yet sold, John shifted in his seat, closed his open notebook, and said, "How do you see this happening, exactly? Last night I couldn't get Teddy Horne on the record about Gus... Now you want me to make his boss change political parties?"

"See that's the thing."

"What's the thing?"

"I'm in the 'what' business... I pay smart people like you to be in the 'how' business."

"You pay me to write."

"Johnny boy, I pay you more for your little freelance column than I pay my editors, right?"

"Yes."

"And I'm pretty sure Teddy Horne over there is probably paying you under the table while letting you drink for free, for positive press for Gus. Right?"

"How did—"

Robert laid down his trump card, "So if I were to fire you, you'd lose both checks."

"Wha—"

"Don't make that face, John. I'm not threatening you. Think of it this way... You're a writer, and in this narrative, I just gave your character some of what's called, 'motivation'."

John dropped his gaze, accepting his fate.

Pressing his advantage, Robert said, "You're covering the stadium opening this week, right?"

"Yeah."

"Gus took out two full page ads in the Courier... So I *too* am in the baseball business this week. I'm thinking instead of just doing the gossip stuff, you should go deeper."

Now puzzled, John asked, "Deeper?"

"First black man to open his own stadium... It's undeniably historic. Let's see if we can give it a little poetry."

"Poetry?"

Robert, smiling, reasserted himself, his title justifying his tone.

"Gus is giving a press conference this afternoon. You should go."

"Okay?"

"Your press credentials have already been typed and are on your desk. Go. Then get to the stadium and interview some of the players on the team like Jud Williams and Joe Wilson."

"You mean Jud Wilson and Joe Williams," John's comment was made funny because the latter wasn't even on the Crawfords, he was still a player on the Homestead Greys.

Robert hated being corrected, especially with details he finds irrelevant. "Whatever... They've got the same initials, they're both big in the south, and I bet even their fans have a hard time telling them apart."

John chuckled as he stood up, closing his jacket.

Robert quipped, "What's so funny?" as John exited the office.

John responded over his shoulder, "Just thinking the same could be said for Jim Crow and Jesus Christ."

Chapter 3

"So, this is what Gus is doing with his money... I should have asked for more."

Leroy Robert Paige, nicknamed "Satchel", stepped out of his brown Cadillac convertible,which he had arrogantly parked in front of Greenlee Field. The only thing shinier than his car were the mahogany leather shoes that matched the Caddy a little too well.

Having risen from below humble beginnings in Mobile, Alabama, Satchel Paige was a rockstar before the term existed.

Knowing Gus Greenlee's considerable cash flow, Satchel had no doubt Greenlee Field could be built in time. He remained unprepared to see it for the first time.

Paige wasn't a stranger to cultural pride, but it normally took a back seat to finance. Now that the finance had been covered, he allowed himself a moment to bask in the shadow of this dream un-deferred.

After walking past security guards at the front entrance, Satchel continued to take in the sights, overpowered by the scent of freshly painted white walls. That was to be expected, preparations would continue right up until Saturday's game.

Once through the main entrance, Paige continued through two short adjoining hallways to a dugout. After climbing the few short steps from the dugout, he was hit by magnitude of Greenlee Field.

The Pittsburgh Crawfords were well into their practice and drills, getting ready for their season opener against the Black Yankees.

A familiar face had just taken the batter's box for hitting practice. Josh Gibson took two nonchalant swings, seemingly to wake up his wrists and forearms, then nodded to the pitcher, as if to say "I'm ready."

CRACK!

Over the right-field wall.

CRACK!

Over the left-field wall.

A voice from the dugout called out, "Boy... That one was *pretty!*"

Josh quipped, "Satchel, the first one was *pretty* too. Where're you coming from? Practice started hours ago, old man."

CRACK!

Satchel continued, talking to Josh while looking everywhere else, "I don't remember. Someplace where someone paid me a whole lotta money, so I struck out a whole lotta batters. Now I'm here, cause Gus is paying me a pretty chunk of change to show up and strike out a bunch of Black Yankees tomorrow. You're welcome."

CRACK!

The other players who were still doing drills and running laps were now focused on home plate, as Josh continued to put on a hitting clinic.

CRACK!!

Satchel now focused on Josh... "You weren't hitting bombs like that last time I saw you in Mexico."

"Oh? Well I found that if I just slide my left foot out about two more inches or so, I can push off my back foot, swing my hips a little harder and just..."

CRACK!!!

The other players had stopped working out, and gathered in awe as ball after ball sailed over different sections of the wall in the outfield.

"Say, you keep hitting em' outta here like that there won't be any left for the other guys to use during practice."

"Huh?"

"Josh, stop punishing the balls and take a walk with me..."

Josh held up his hand, signalling to the pitcher that he was stepping out of the batter's box. The other players on the field applauded and cheered. He tipped his cap.

As the two men walked toward the dugout, Satchel resumed their conversation from before.

"Why are they telling me you're not my catcher tomorrow?"

"Yeah, got me in left field... Appendix surgery. Doctor's orders: Pain meds and no crouching for two weeks."

"Pain meds?" Satchel himself looked pained.

"I have a prescription for them... In fact when I leave here I'm heading straight to the pharmacy, big bro."

"Well, I guess as long as your bat is in the lineup..."

"We'll be good."

"Good? Shiiiiiii... Listen negro, money can't get any smarter than when you bet it on this cannon I got hanging off this here right shoulder."

Josh smiled and nodded.

Wide-eyed, Satchel continued to marvel at the dugout. "Man... Gus built the hell outta this here park."

"It's nice to be able to shower where we sweat and not have to hose each other off around the corner... Which is ideal 'cause you work up a funk there, Satch."

Satchel shrugged off the insult, "I ain't done nothin' half way since I was a tike!"

Both men laughed.

Paige continued, "But seriously, Gus outdid himself with all this. Looks like history is happening right in front of— hold up, now."

Josh had taken off his cap and was beginning to toss it on the bench to cool off. Satchel tried to stop him.

It was too late.

Josh, curious, "What's wrong?"

"The paint is still wet... Can't you smell it?"

Josh picked up his ball cap, noticing a large white paint stain on the underside of the bill.

"You know Gus is gonna make you wear a new one tomorrow, and if memory serves, you like to wear the same hat for 24 hours before you play."

Josh continued to inspect his ballcap, "Satchel, don't even start. Now get outta my way so I can get to the pharmacy before they close. Meet you at the Grill later?”

“Yeah.”

“Okay…” Josh turned to head to the hallways away from the field. “Oh, and Satchel?”

“Yeah, Josh?”

“I make my own luck.”

Satchel quickly replied but only to himself, “Said no ballplayer ever.”

Chapter 4

Back at the Pittsburgh Courier, when John received his marching orders from Robert, he casually walked out of the office as a mild form of protest. But once out the door, he wasted no time getting downstairs and over the few short blocks to the tailor's entrance of Sam Reznik & Sons, where the spectacle of the crowd was hard to miss. Reporters and photographers clamored, cameras flashing in a consistent cadence as John entered.

He did his best to not be offended when a skinny, short kid who had seen him countless times with Gus, wordlessly held out his hand. Nevertheless, John handed over his credentials and entered.

Teenie, a black man in his early twenties working as a press photographer for the Pittsburgh Courier, recognized John and flagged him over.

Cameras flashed as Gus Greenlee, a husky, fair-skinned black man in his late thirties, stood at the center of this orchestrated chaos, while getting fitted for a white suit. His security was close by. Teddy stood near, and Brick guarded the door. A velvet rope separated them from reporters.

One called out, "I hear Josh Gibson is injured? Will he be playing tomorrow?"

Gus laughed off the question, "Josh Gibson is most certainly in the lineup. I did hear something about him being in the outfield."

"Why won't he be catching?" another reporter asked.

Gus responded, camera flashes punctuating his words, "I'm not the manager... I just get the manager what he needs to win. You'll have to ask him."

"You've got a pricey roster, sir," another reporter noted.

"Do I?" Gus feigned shock, looking to Teddy for faux confirmation. Another flash. Teddy, not one to shy away from improvised comedy, shrugged, "It's not my money."

Another reporter pressed, "Whadaya say to people who claim you're jeopardizing the soul of the game?"

Gus smirked, "Hmm. Well, I'd tell *Cumberland Posey*, nobody ever built a legacy on the cheap. I'm trying to make American Negro history right before everyone's very eyes. And I'd tell him that he should have paid his talent better."

As the back-and-forth banter unfolded, Marion Frank, a black man in his late forties with chemically straightened, but messy black hair, appeared.

The kid checking press credentials looked at him and was about to stick out his hand, when Brick, who'd been eyeing a lemon yellow dress hanging behind the counter, noticed Marion and rushed over to intervene.

It was clear Marion had been up all night.

Brick leaned over to whisper, "Mr. Frank... You okay?"

John noted the exchange, but returned his attention to the press conference.

"Who will you be supporting for President this year?" another reporter boldly inquired.

Gus looked baffled, and with a hushed tone only audible to Teddy, muttered, "...The fuck did he just ask me?"

"We're only answering baseball questions today," Teddy interjected, addressing the reporter. No sign of improvised comedy there.

Gus was now weary of his own vanity exercise.

"I'm surprised you all aren't asking me more about this stadium. It's the first one designed, built, and owned by Negroes. That's right, even the architect was black.

And I'm hoping it's not the last. We're gonna have everything they got in their stadiums, you hear me? Can't wait to see you all there." The statement was an obvious sign off. Gus stepped back on the fitting block and faced the mirror;the tailor returned to his hem.

But for those who still needed to hear the words, Teddy offered, "Uh, guys, we're gonna need the room. That's all the questions for today. Make sure you all come by the Grill to get your complimentary tickets and passes... We're making history tomorrow, folks."

The reporters, including John and Teenie, filed out. Outside, John paused, and under his breath asked Brick, "Who's that?" referring to Marion Frank.

Brick responded cryptically, "You never saw him... Keep walking, Clarke." Once everyone was out, Teddy approached Gus.

Gus started, "Who's that? He looks familiar."

"Former Pittsburgh heavyweight champion from 1924 to 1927. And he's the father of one of the girls who works the Grill with Lena." Gus's expression turned serious. "You check him for a piece?"

"Brick did," Teddy assured.

Marion, tense and anxious, approached Gus as the last of the reporters left the shop. "Sir... I know you're a busy man. And I wouldn't have come to you except—"

Gus cut him off, "Always have time for the Crawford family. I think I remember seeing you fight a few times. You okay? You look like you had a long night."

Marion looked in the mirror and attempted to comb his hair with his hands, a moment of vanity in his crisis. "It's my daughter Marie. I talked to her on the phone last night before her shift ended. But she never came home... My wife and I have looked everywhere, I mean, she doesn't get into trouble. This isn't like her."

Because he was a man of about 6 foot 3 inches, 245 pounds, and with musculature more dense than even Brick, the fact that Marion's voice cracked exhibited his vulnerability. A man who towered over everyone in that room had begun to grieve the loss of his daughter. And he felt small. So small.

Gus glanced at Brick, who seemed momentarily taken aback, then nodded silently. "Brick, can you bring us some ice water?" Brick, himself fighting back tears, moved to fetch the water.

Gus asked, "Teddy, what time did she leave last night?"

"We clocked her out after 11," Teddy answered.

Gus's face hardened with resolve. "From now on, get someone to drive the girls home after their shift, 'till I say otherwise."

He waved the tailor away, stepping down from the fitting block to face Marion more directly, and signaled for Teddy to stand near. "Teddy Horne here is my best guy. His daughter, Lena, even works at the Grill from time to time," Gus explained, making eye contact with Teddy to emphasize the gravity of the situation. "This is now his highest priority."

Gus's tone softened but remained firm. "After we finish this conversation, Brick here is gonna drive you home, where you will tell your wife you talked to me. And that I said you'll both have answers as quickly as I can get them."

Marion nodded, relief and gratitude mixing in his tired eyes. "Thank you, sir...," he managed to say, voice thick with emotion.

Gus's expression was unreadable now as he concluded, "Now start from the beginning and tell us everything you already know..."

Chapter 5

Jeff Lee, Bobby Davis, Riley Malone, and George Walsh.

All pissed off.

But they were gaining little ground in a heated argument with their now-former foreman about having been laid off. Michael, within earshot, couldn't help but overhear.

"You can't do this to us. Some of us have newborns at home," George shouted at the foreman, his voice echoing off the concrete walls.

"I know... And I'm sorry abou—" the foreman started.

Bobby interjected angrily with, "You *should* be sorry about sending *us* home... While *THEY* get to stay!"

"They?"

Jeff pointed accusingly at Michael, who was quietly continuing his work.

"He seems to still have his job? I mean… It ain't right. Sending white men home while you're keeping these—" Jeff's voice was thick with resentment.

The foreman cut in, trying to explain, "Listen guys… The union pushed us for those raises."

"We earned those raises," George asserted.

"Hell yeah we did," Riley added, nodding vigorously.

"Well, anyway,they did, and they set your salaries a little too high last year for us to continue with diminishing sales, and guys like Mike over there aren't in the union," the foreman explained, voice strained.

Bobby, increasingly agitated, blurted, "I mean it feels like you're punishing us for not being colored!" His face was red with anger and frustration.

Michael, trying to maintain his composure, closed his eyes and said another prayer amidst the escalating tension.

"So you're saying there's nothing we can do?" asked Riley.

"I guess you can find us somebody to sell more steel to… You don't have any rich uncles building a skyscraper downtown, do ya?"

The foreman, realizing his humor was wasted in this moment, adopted a firmer tone. "You all come in here, cursing at me, in the same clothes you wore yesterday... and smelling like pond scum took a shit on you... Isn't helping your cause.

Now, I know you guys need to blow off steam. Boys will be boys, right? But that guy over there is on time, does his job, and only takes home half of what you make. In what way do you think this is a hard decision?"

Bobby clenched his fist and leaned forward menacingly, but Jeff caught him. "Bobby... Let's just go. Don't wanna make it so we can never come back."

"Yeah... Listen to your pal. Clearly he's the brains of your little operation," the foreman quipped as they walked out, Bobby bumping Michael's shoulder and making deliberate eye contact as he passed. A silent dare for him to react. Michael held his peace, though his lower back spasmed from the impact.

After the others left, the foreman walked to Michael. "Sorry about that, Mike."

"That's okay, sir."

"How's the back?"

"Never better," Michael lied, a slight wince betraying his pain.

The foreman chuckled, sensing the lie. "Should've seen that lie coming."

Michael laughed, "Then why'd you ask?"

"I honestly don't know. Listen, you still got a job but you're off the clock. The economy is swirling down the toilet... There are fewer buildings being built. When they don't need steel, the mill doesn't need either of us," the foreman explained somberly.

Michael nodded, understanding the gravity of the situation.

"And I'm gonna need the people who do show up to be as close to 100% as possible. When's the last time you spent time with your kids?"

"I see them at night," Michael said, quietly.

"Go spend some time with them," the foreman advised, his voice carrying a mix of concern and command. "Listen, Jeff and Bobby are just two of 15 guys we had to let go. Add that to the fact they know who we're not letting go... probably getting drunk across the street right now... and I'd sleep better knowing you guys took a few days off... for safety."

"But I—" Michael began to protest.

"It's done! Seriously, I'm not gonna dock your pay for today, but for right now? I want you to get to a doctor... Get some happy pills or something and put your feet up. Come back next week ready to give me the same effort that kept you here," the foreman said firmly.

Michael conceded, hung up his sledge hammer, and limped over to pick up his cane.

Chapter 6

The setting sun cast long shadows across the Hill District as Mac walked home; his hand-painted jersey hung loosely, unbuttoned, and the brim of his cap shaded his eyes. One hand gripped his catcher's mitt while balancing his bat on his shoulder; the other held tight to his 5-year-old sister Missy's hand. They crossed the street together.

Missy offered an almost minute-to-minute account of her day as they walked. Mac didn't mind — it was better than remembering his own day.

"...then Mrs. Frank made all of us kids take a second nap."

"A second nap?" Mac asked, a hint of amusement in his voice.

"The nerve! I mean it was story time, and I was

the one sitting with the book in the big red rocking chair... In the middle of Little Red Riding Hood, right as the Big Bad Wolf gets to Grandma's house... The best part of the story if you ask me... Mrs. Frank started crying... And told us all to lay down," Missy explained.

"Crying? Why?" Mac's tone shifted to concern.

"Something about her daughter. She was SO sad."

"Oh..." Mac's response was soft, thoughtful.

Missy took a beat before changing the subject to something closer to her heart. "How did you play?"

Mac sighed, the day's disappointments briefly crossing his face. "Oh for three with a fly out in the ninth to end the game."

"Ouchie," Missy winced sympathetically.

"Left the tying run on third," Mac added, the sting of the game still fresh.

"Double ouchie," Missy remarked, squeezing his hand slightly.

"Yup," Mac said as they approached their modest tenement building. He quickly checked the mail before opening the door, allowing her to enter first.

"Go get cleaned up, I'll get some soup started," Mac directed, taking on the role of caretaker.

"Okay... Mac?" Missy paused at the doorway, her voice small.

"Yeah, Missy?" Mac turned, attentive.

"It's okay, there's always tomorrow," she said.

"Your impression of Ma is getting better," Mac responded with a soft chuckle, meant to mask the undercurrent of their shared longing.

"I miss her..." Missy's voice was a whisper now.

"Me too," Mac agreed, his voice barely above a murmur as he kissed her forehead gently.

Once inside, Mac slid off his shirt and dropped it into a washtub in the kitchen. Then he washed his hands with the bar soap his father's soot-covered hands made darker after every use.

Mac started the family dinner.

40

Chapter 7

As the sun went down outside, the desk lamps inside the Pittsburgh Courier office seemed to grow brighter.

John and Teenie sat with their feet propped up on the desk as the room filled with lazy swirls of cigarette smoke. The two men shared a quiet moment, reflecting on the day's events.

"So he literally said the word *poetry*?" Teenie asked, disbelief coloring his tone.

"He did," John confirmed, flicking ash into a nearby tray.

"He expecting a sonnet?" Teenie joked, with a wry smile.

"I guess," John shrugged, his mind still wrapped

around the assignment.

"Of Pittsburgh?" Teenie prodded further, amusement evident in his voice.

"Well, the Hill specifically — I suppose — but incorporating the stadium and opening day. Something with a message... A theme, even." John mused.

"Well, let me know what you want a picture of..." Teenie offered, ready to capture whatever John needed in order to complement his writing.

"Honestly? What I really want is a picture of something that will make Gus back the Roosevelt who's running as a Democrat," John admitted, his expression serious despite the unlikely nature of his wish.

"Oh... Sorry, no go there, he's pretty clean for a gangster," Teenie responded, an edge of respect in his tone for their subject's cautious conduct.

"Wait, I didn't — you thought I wanted you to take blackmail pictures of the biggest gangster in town?" John clarified, surprised by the misunderstanding.

"No. I'm saying I tried to do it for free... For me. You never know when you may need 'em," Teenie admitted, revealing a layer of pragmatism beneath his jovial demeanor.

"Fascinating. And Gus is..." John prompted, intrigued by this new angle.

"Clean as a whistle. I mean, aside from the numbers.

The dude doesn't even have a personal life, I could find," Teenie disclosed, almost admiringly.

"Hmm, how about that? Say... You know who the guy was tha—" John started to ask, a previous curiosity resurfacing.

"Marion Frank, former boxer, regional Heavyweight champ from '24 to '27," Teenie cut in, answering before John could finish his question.

"That's where I knew him from..." John snapped his fingers, the connection finally clicking.

"I went to school with his daughter Marie." Teenie paused to whistle, exposing his own childhood crush on her, then continued, "His wife Dihanne runs a school for young children out of their home."

"Marie? Why is that name familia—" John's mind drifted away as if solving a math problem in his head.

"—She has a big red rocking chair that she lets the kids read from during story time. Sitting in that chair as a kid was the first time many of us felt like we could be somebody," Teenie recalled.

It snapped for him!

"Marie!!! The girl who just started working at Gus's Crawford Grill... Her name is Marie... Hmmmm."

"Any reason why he'd be running to Gus though?" John queried, trying to piece together Marion's unexpected presence at the tailor shop.

"I think if we were meant to know that, they wouldn't have kicked us out," Teenie reasoned, his tone suggesting that some secrets in the Hill weren't meant for him.

The journalist in John was instantly disappointed in Teenie's lack of interest; however, as a man, John completely understood his pragmatism.

"You're smarter than you look," John remarked, half-teasing.

"I get that a lot... Say... You hungry?"

Chapter 8

The sun had adopted that "final few hours before punching out" posture that Michael — in his own way - knew all too well.

His painful shuffle from earlier in the day was now a crippled waddle down Wylie Avenue. His cane, now a necessity.

And yet with sheer determination and a little faith in the potential power of narcotic-based relief, Michael endured his pain to reach Crampton's Drugs, the neighborhood pharmacy.

Pushing the door open, he heard a bell ring overhead. A fair skinned black man peered from behind a counter at the back of the establishment, about 30 feet away.

The distance wouldn't have seemed much to anyone

else, but with Michael's labored mobility, he saw the effort required as herculean. Each step required more of his dedication and will than it should.

The pharmacist looked both concerned for Michael's pain, but impatient at the amount of time it was taking. He wasn't encouraged by Michael's worn down exterior.

At that moment, the sound of a toilet flushing came from the men's room, and shortly after, Josh Gibson emerged. His appearance was also a bit disheveled; jersey unbuttoned, hat stained, right-hand pressed against his stomach, signaling distress.

Patiently, Josh took his place in line behind Michael, who was almost at the rear counter.

"Can I help you?" the pharmacist inquired, his tone professional yet distant.

"Hi. I pulled my back at work something terrible. I was told to ask you for some 'happy pills' but I didn't know what that meant," Michael explained, his voice strained with discomfort.

Josh's attention sharpened, drawn by Michael's mention of his ailment.

"Tell me more about this back pain. Have you sat in a warm tub?" the pharmacist asked, suggesting conventional remedies.

Michael, struggling to maintain his posture, shook his head wearily. "Well... I let Shep at the church look at it... And I did the stretches he told me to do but it doesn't seem to help," he confessed.

At that moment Josh's empathy for Michael's pain turned to impatience with the pharmacist. Thinking to himself, "How can you see someone in that much pain and stick to some cold script." Josh remembered his life before he hit baseballs record distances. The fact that *he* was also in pain didn't help.

Josh felt compelled to interject, "Damn Doc... The man told you what he needed..."

Michael turned to see who had spoken on his behalf, meeting Josh's earnest gaze.

The pharmacist, constrained by regulations, responded cautiously, "I understand, but with no prescription... I have a license to protect, this is how I feed my family."

Josh, realizing the complexity of Michael's situation, apologized, "Shit... Alright... I'm sorry, man..."

Michael, taken aback by the unexpected advocacy, remained speechless.

Josh, looking to resolve his own needs, politely asked, "Well, do you mind? I actually do have a script for my meds..."

Michael stepped aside, allowing Josh to proceed. He cast lingering glances over his shoulder as he exited the pharmacy slowly, as if giving the pharmacist an opportunity to reconsider.

The pharmacist never did.

Josh handed over a crumpled prescription, his voice carrying a mixture of urgency and relief, "I need a refill."

The pharmacist nodded, "I'll be right back."

While waiting, Josh heard the bell on the front door of the store ring. Michael had left. Defeated.

With its shift now completely over, the sun headed west, leaving Pittsburgh's Hill district,especially Wylie Avenue, dark. Michael had 10 more blocks to get home. He'd used that day's budgeted 5-cent bus fare to see Mac play in the afternoon. It was worth it, despite the result.

Josh, having just exited the pharmacy, walked past the Crawford Grill (located conveniently next door), noticed Michael struggling, and called out to him. "Hey, hold on, pal!"

Michael turned to the sound of a man jogging toward him. He gripped his cane tighter to use as a potential weapon, until he saw the voice's owner.

"Listen, man... I feel terrible about what happened in there... How'd you hurt yourself?" Josh asked, stepping closer to minimize the distance between them.

"Trynna put food on the table," Michael responded with a weary half-smile.

"How heavy is that food?" Josh joked, attempting to lighten the mood.

Michael chuckled. "...At the steel mill."

"I knew what you meant... Say, what do people call you?" Josh asked, shifting the conversation to a more personal level.

"My friends call me Mike," Michael replied, extending his hand for a firm shake.

"Hi, Mike... I'm—" Josh started to introduce himself.

"My son's hero..." Michael interjected, a mix of pride and surprise in his voice.

Josh, taken aback by the comment, paused. "Oh?"

"Seventy-some odd home runs last year alone," Michael continued, his voice filled with admiration. "My kid plays catcher like you... He makes me throw him a hundred pitches — in this condition — every Sunday afternoon for batting practice... He crouches like a catcher listening to your games on the radio, and even hand-painted your number on his uniform."

Josh turned away, a smile breaking across his face as he processed the compliment. "Eh... How about that..."

"Today at lunch, I hopped two buses to see him play his first game as a starter..." Michael's voice trailed off as he recalled the moment.

"How'd he do?" Josh inquired, genuinely interested.

"Flied out to center, bottom of the 9th. It crushed him," Michael replied, pride evident even in the recount of a loss.

"Oooh... Ouch. Probably feels like he let his team down?" Josh sympathized, understanding the weight of such moments.

"Yeah, but for a kid his age — let's just say he held it together. Hell, he holds everything together. Anyway, I didn't want him to see me, in case..." Michael's voice faltered, hinting at the layers of personal struggle behind his stoic façade.

"Yeah, I know... Man, I know. Never want to add to the pressure," Josh nodded, his tone softening.

"But if anyone asks him about the Yankees, he'll tell 'em they play alright with number 3 being the white Josh Gibson, but imagine how good they'd be if they had the *real* Josh Gibson on the team," Michael added, a light chuckle escaping him despite the pain.

Josh laughed, humbled by the admiration. "Does he now? That's pretty kind of him..."

"Thanks for giving him someone to, um..." Michael looked away to steady himself, "...Look up to."

Josh felt the weight of that compliment deeply. "Wow... Umm... Just wow..."

Taking a moment to collect himself, Josh said, "So, uh, listen. I just had appendix surgery, so I've got an unlimited supply of these coming to me." He reached into his pocket, pulling out a small paper bag.

"I can't..." Michael protested.

"Nah... There's only ten in there, and no doctor around here is gonna be open tonight. So take two of these and actually get some rest," Josh insisted, pushing the bag into Michael's hand.

"You don't drink liquor, do ya?"

"Not in a while."

"Good... You can't do that with these."

"Okay."

"But you gotta talk to someone about that back. It doesn't get better by ignoring it..."

Michael, shocked but grateful, nodded. "Yes, sir."

"Be careful... And be close to a bed when you take them. Because whenever they kick in, it's gonna be bedtime," Josh said with a hint of humor.

"Ha... Thanks... Oh, and give them Black Yankees hell tomorrow," Michael said, managing a smile.

"I'll try!" Josh answered, clearly moved by the encounter.

As both men turned to leave, Josh paused. "Oh,you know what? Give your son this..." He took off his baseball cap, then pulled out a pen.

"Huh?" Michael was startled.

"The white paint stain means I can't wear it in the game tomorrow. Your son... What's his name?"

"McGray... My late wife's maiden name," Michael answered, voice thick with emotion.

"Man, I'm sorry... I'm also a wid— You all call him Mac?"

"Yeah, we do."

Josh scribbled an autograph on the cap.

"Good strong name," Josh said, handing the cap back to Michael. "Say... You hopped two buses, in your condition, just to see him play ball in a hand-painted shirt?"

"Yeah..." Michael confirmed, looking down at his shoes.

"Don't sell yourself short," Josh advised earnestly. "Your son already had someone to look up to. Next time let him see you."

Chapter 9

"For thine is the power
and the glory
for ever and ever… Amen"

A group of parents seated around a backyard picnic table erupted in exuberant applause. Allison, 6, Riley Jr., 5, and Melissa, 4, smiled after having recited The Lord's Prayer from memory.

Spring evenings like this were for family Bible recitations, especially for the homeschooled children of Riley Malone and George Walsh.

Both raised in West Virginia, Riley and George were each named after their grandfathers, who met while wearing blue at the start of the Civil War.

The Malone and Walsh families were so close that during World War I, Riley and George enlisted together, served together, and came home to marry their respective high school sweethearts a week apart.

(While it had been discussed, their wives vehemently refused to share a wedding day.)

So no one who knew them was surprised when "Riles" and "Georgey" chose to buy adjacent plots of land in suburban Pittsburgh on which to build adjoining houses.

They chose Pittsburgh because the coal industry seemed to offer consistent employment and upward mobility for family men.

Even though their families had fought for the country on two separate occasions, because of their Irish last names, they were overlooked until their American accents led employers or loan officers to give them the benefit of the doubt.

Truth be told, that's how their grandfathers were paired together years ago in basic training. No one else wanted to pair up with them.

In 1929 came the Crash.

Then the first three years of the Great Depression to follow hadn't quite hit them until yesterday.

And while their prospects and savings were sure to dwindle, their mortgage notes surely would not.

So they took the only jobs available: steel mill 7am-

7pm shift.

The back-breaking work was rough, but somehow working with your best friend made it bearable, even through the crazy shift hours.

Their wives, having also grown up as best friends, took turns homeschooling the children and running errands during the day.

After the recital of the Psalm, the two families ate dinner together outside.

On the radio, Riley Jr. heard there was a big baseball game tomorrow involving some team called the Crawfords, and wanted to go. His mother shut that down with a quick, "That's not for you."

Riley Jr. shrugged, then went right back to eating his hamburger.

Once dinner was finished, Riley and George smoked cigars and drank beers on the back porch while their wives and children cleaned the table. There was no talk of dessert, but it was Friday night, so the odds were good. Homemade ice cream... And pie made with apples plucked from trees on the property.

Riley's wife hinted that the mill should be giving out their spring bonus soon... And if not that, aren't the two men at least due for a raise?

As if cued by an orchestra conductor, crickets in the yard chirped loudly to fill the awkward pause before George spoke up, "When we know, darlin', you'll know. So don't go spending it just yet..."

Both women laughed, and in unison, almost like school girls, said, "We'll try."

The doorbell rang.

Elle, George's wife, went to see who it was.

Riley and George made instant eye contact, aware that no bullets were dodged, only slowed.

They continued smoking among the chorus of crickets, sipping their beers as Jeff and Bobby came out the back door of the house to join them.

The four men had become friends last year when Jeff and Bobby joined the 7–7 shift.

As Southerners, Jeff and Bobby spoke with accents which made them as undesirable as the "Irish in name only" George and Riley. They occasionally joked that their grandfathers could very well have shot at each other during the "war of northern aggression." But they were bigger people for having bonded beyond those battle lines.

So as a team of misfits they bonded. They'd hunt and fish together.

And now they'd all collectively decided not to tell their wives their updated employment status.

Jeff handed George and Riley each a thin envelope with a few dollars.

"Its not much but Bobby and I came into a little

money the other night; gambling. We figured every little bit helps, right?"

The West Virginians accepted the cash, now knowing when or where their next dollar would materialize.

George noticed a scratch on the side of Jeff's face he hadn't seen this afternoon. "Jeff, how'd you get that scratch?"

"Oh it's nothing... You know that shed I've got over there near Myers pond?"

"Yeah."

"I got into a scrape with some kind of raccoon over there," Jeff said, making eye contact with Bobby.

George moved on. Taking a long drag from his cigar, he offered, "The traffic patterns around the colored section of town are changing..."

Jeff asked, "Why?" with a little more intent than usual.

George responded, "The new baseball stadium is opening."

Bobby asked, "On the *Hill*?"

Riley added, "And not just anywhere either... Where the Entress Brick Company used to be."

Jeff reflected, "That was my first job..."

George inquired, "How are your wives handling the news?"

Bobby looked around and said, "What news?"

The men chuckled awkwardly.

Riley questioned, "Who's the new union rep?"

Jeff replied, "I think it's Dick Martin, but he isn't taking any calls. Plus I think he got demoted to only half shifts himself."

Bobby asked, "What are we gonna do?"

Jeff queried further, "Who'd you say built that new stadium? Maybe we can get him to buy some steel and get our jobs back…"

Chapter 10

Inside the Crawford Grill, the atmosphere was alive with a vibrant and integrated crowd. Black and white patrons mingled freely; after all, in that room everyone broke the law.

Laughter and spirited discussions blended with the backdrop of music that filled the air; loud enough to be heard, yet subdued enough to allow conversations to dominate.

At the bar, Gus Greenlee, the proprietor, was busy attending to a special guest, M.E. Goodson, a shorter black man in his late fifties, distinguished in his suit and fedora. Goodson seemed quite interested in Janet, the newest waitress, who was on shift that night. Gus had already seen to it that his personal driver pick her up from her home and would be the one to take her back at the end of the night.

Gus couldn't blame Goodson for looking. Janet turned heads each time she crossed the room. But with Marie still missing, and Lena not due back for weeks, Janet was the only person he trusted to open the Grill tomorrow during the game. Goodson was going to have to pick someone else, if he wanted *company.*

Goodson was a barber and cabaret owner back in Harlem. But he was in Pittsburgh as the owner of the Black Yankees. It was his team due to play Greenlee's Crawfords on opening day.

Gus and Goodson discussed a few last-minute logistics. "You know, if we'd played this game in the Bronx, we could have played it at night."

Gus, pouring drinks, replied without missing a beat, "But the guys wouldn't be allowed to use the showers or even the locker room."

"I'm just saying the fans like night games," Goodson persisted.

"Talk to me when you have to pay to install your own lights," Gus retorted, his tone half-joking yet pointed. Don't try to out-boss a boss.

"Well, last order of business on the list. We won't need a batboy," Goodson added, changing the subject.

Gus looked up, confused for a moment. "Huh?"

"Some ball clubs provide them for visiting teams. I'm just saying we have one of our own. He's the son of one of the guys on the team. We won a couple exhibition games with this kid managing the equipment... The guys are superstitious, so we kind of kept the kid around. We pay him 50 cents," Goodson explained, his voice filled with a mix of practicality and amusement at his players' superstitions.

"Oh... Of course, that's fine," Gus nodded, his mind already moving to the next matter.

At that moment, Brick entered the bar. Gus waved him over and stepped aside to speak privately.

"Yes sir," Brick greeted him, ready for instructions.

"You hearing anything from Teddy?" Gus asked, his voice low and concerned.

"We've got most of our guys on the street right now with a picture of Marie, but nothing yet," Brick reported, his tone serious.

"Alright... I want updates. Regularly," Gus instructed.

"Will do," Brick affirmed, ready to continue the search.

Gus, suddenly remembering another oversight, added, "Cool... Oh... In all the haste getting ready for today, I forgot to hire a batboy."

"You forgot?" Brick asked, slightly amused yet surprised.

"I mean I've had a few things on my mind. You got a son?" Gus inquired, already thinking ahead.

"Not yet," Brick responded.

As Goodson approached again, clearing his throat to signal his presence, Gus addressed him, "Yeah... Give me another minute."

Reaching beneath the bar, Gus pulled out an envelope full of tickets he had held for the team, in case they wanted to invite family and friends. He instructed Brick, "Give this to Satchel, then tell him to find us a batboy. I'm paying 50 cents." As Goodson cleared his throat even louder, Gus, not appreciating the passive-aggressive approach, shot back, "Excuse me... Does that [fake coughs] shit work in Harlem?"

Brick handed the envelope of tickets to Satchel, who had just walked in, and asked him if he knew anyone who could be a good batboy to the tune of two quarters. "Of course I do. I know everyone and everyone knows me," Satchel responded confidently.

Janet walked by.

Satchel turned to Brick, intrigued, "Uhh, Brick... Who's that?"

Chapter 11

By the time Michael had walked the full distance to his apartment building and climbed the stairs to the unit he was grateful to have, the Morrison apartment was enveloped in darkness save for a solitary light illuminating the kitchen.

As he stepped inside, his eyes quickly adjusted to the dim lighting, he caught sight of a recently cleaned jersey hanging to dry over a radiator. Nearby, a pot of soup simmered gently on the stove, filling the space with a warm, inviting aroma.

The kid's cooking is getting better.

Just then, Mac walked into the room, breaking the stillness. "Hey Dad," he greeted, his voice carrying the mix of exhaustion and disappointment of someone way older.

"Hey Mac..." Michael paused, searching for the right words. "So um, how was the game?"

Mac's head hung slightly lower, his shoulders slumped as he confessed, "We lost... I had a chance to— we lost."

Michael stepped closer, placing a comforting hand on his son's shoulder. "Hey listen buddy. Everyone has good days... And everyone has some bad days, but remember as long as there's a tomorrow you can make it anything you want it to be."

Mac, still grappling with his disappointment, countered, "Josh Gibson would have hit a homer, he never has bad days..."

Michael chuckled softly, trying to impart a bit of wisdom. "Of course he does. I'm sure of it."

"How do you know?" Mac challenged.

"'Cause last I checked he was included in 'everyone,'" Michael replied, his tone gentle yet firm.

Mac let out a laugh. His dad had a point.

Seizing the moment, Michael added, "Also, while I'm thinking about it, he asked me to give you this." He reached under his arm and pulled out the ball cap that Josh had autographed.

Mac's eyes widened in disbelief. "NO, he didn't..."

"Yeah... He signed the inside just in case you said that," Michael said, his voice soaked with pride.

Mac took the hat, turning it over in his hands to examine the autograph. Instantly the cap became his most prized possession.

Mac looked up at his father, speechless.

Chapter 12

Within the Frank household, the atmosphere was thick with tension and sorrow. Diahann, in her late forties, sat at the kitchen bar, her day's distress etched clearly across her face.

Mascara tracks stained her cheeks. Her hands trembled as she attempted to pour yet another three fingers of whiskey into her overused glass. Her movements were clumsy from a combination of emotion and the inebriation she needed to cope with those emotions.

Marion, her husband, approached gently, his voice soft yet fraught with concern. "Baby…"

"Don't *baby* me," Diahann snapped back, her voice cracking under the strain. She paused, her eyes fierce and searching as she implored, "*Where* is she?"

"I told you," Marion began, trying to offer reassurance amidst the storm of her despair.

"FIND HER!" Diahann's voice rose, a desperate plea mixed with a command.

"Ba— ...Diahann... Gus has an army of men that can do things we can't... He told me he'll send someone over here as soon as they have answers."

Diahann's anguish was palpable as she countered, "This wouldn't have happened if she weren't *working* for Gus. My child is out there somewhere, and you want me to gamble her safety with the neighborhood numbers guy?"

Marion, options limited, responded with a harsh reality. "You'd rather I go and get ignored at the police station?"

The truth of Marion's words struck Diahann hard, but they did little to soothe her torment.

In a fit of rage and despair, she hurled her drink at the bar, where bottles of illegal alcohol lined the shelves. The glass shattered the mirror, reflecting the jagged brokenness she felt internally.

Chapter 13

At the now-empty Pittsburgh Courier office, John was almost ready to go home. He packed up his briefcase with office supplies he probably didn't need to steal.

Teenie had left over an hour ago.

But John was chewing on a mystery which hadn't yet been solved.

Suddenly there was a subtle rumbling of keys in the front door lock. John figured it was the janitor, so was surprised when Robert stumbled into the office.

Noticing that John's desk lamp was still on, he straightened his back to perform his best "I'm not drunk" walk toward him.

"How'd it >>hiccup<< go?" Robert attempted to

mask his condition by leaning on an adjacent desk.

John decided not to act confused. He didn't know if drunk Robert was an angry drunk or a happy drunk. Best not to assume.

"It was definitely the vanity exercise we expected, but two questions caught my attention. The first concerned who he would endorse in the upcoming election," John said, setting the stage for the discussion to follow.

"And he said?" Robert leaned forward, intrigued by the potential implications of Gus's political leanings.

"He dodged the question," John replied, a hint of frustration coloring his tone.

Robert's eyebrows rose in surprise, a faint smile playing on his lips. "Hmph, maybe this won't be that hard after all…"

Not fully grasping Robert's implication, John said, "I'm sorry, sir?"

"Never mind. What was the other question?" Robert shifted the topic, keen to gather as much information as possible.

"The other was about the stadium lights," John said.

"Lights?" Robert echoed, interest piqued.

"For night games," John clarified.

"Oh. Hmmm, they don't have lights?" Robert pondered aloud, considering the implications.

"Inside yes, but not on the field," John confirmed.

"Interesting," Robert murmured, his mind already turning over the potential angles for further exploration.

"Then Marion Frank walked in, right?" John continued.

"Marion who?" Robert asked, momentarily caught off guard.

"Wife runs that school for young—" John began to explain.

"Oh, yeah. What did he want?" Robert interrupted, recalling the individual in question.

"Don't know but it was enough to end the press conference. Want me to dig?" John proposed, sensing there might be more beneath the surface of the staged event.

"No, keep it on baseball. I may have Teenie follow this Marion guy, but you had a good day. I might already have what I need. Let me make a few calls." Robert seemed pleased. "Come back to my office, I think I have a bottle of bourbon in there."

John was about to say no, when every synapse in his brain fired at once.

"Marie Franks! The waitress at the Grill. Is Marion's daughter!"

"John, what the hell are you talking about?"

"Nothing... But I have to go," John excused himself and immediately ran out the door.

Robert shrugged, frowned, then wondered why the hell he'd even come back to the office.

Chapter 14

Josh and Satchel found themselves at the end of the bar, each lost in their own thoughts, yet together in the moment. Josh nursed his drink slowly, sipping with a pensiveness that filled the space between them. Satchel, having already downed two of the four shots in front of him, was somewhat distracted by Janet, who was working the room with effortless grace.

Josh broke the silence, his voice low and reflective. "Satch... You ever wonder if there's more to what we are, than baseball?"

Satchel looked up, slightly puzzled by the depth of the question. "Uh... What? Yeah... Well, all I know how to do is play baseball... And talk shit. Both come *au naturale* to me."

"I know, me too," Josh responded, his voice tinged

with a mix of resignation and contemplation.

"And before I played baseball,to the rest of the world, I was just another nigger from Mobile who was known for talking shit," Satchel confessed.

"Elevator operator at Gimbels here, but yeah, me too," Josh offered, though it need not be said.

Satchel furrowed his brow, "So I don't understand your question."

"Do you think we could be doing more?" Josh pressed.

Satchel laughed, in an effort to exit the existential. "Oh... Wait, you gonna become a preacher or something?"

"No," Josh said, quickly dismissing the idea.

"Good, 'cause I'm already at a disadvantage 'cause you ain't catching for me tomorrow. I'd rather you not be out there pondering the meaning of life while you're in the batter's box," Satchel quipped"Yeah, sorry about that," Josh said, and snapped out of his internal thoughts.

Throughout the conversation, he'd been beating himself up. "I shouldn't be mixing these pain pills with alcohol. I *know* better!" Before eventually resolving, "Well, it's too late now."

"But there's a way you can make it up to me," Satchel proposed, sliding an envelope across the bar.

"Make it up to you?" Josh looked surprised but

intrigued.

"Yeah... You can hand out some of these tickets to the guys on the team. You know, their families, and get your son to be batboy. Gus'll pay him 50 cents." Satchel's suggestion came with a hint of playfulness.

"Actually, I haven't seen him in a bit, you see his mother and I... I —," Josh began to overshare.

"You're the best," Satchel interjected, careful not to enter Josh's emotional briar patch.

Satchel stood up and took a few steps, before an impulse hit him to return and go through the envelope full of tickets one more time. Before long he'd found the two seats he was looking for and slid the envelope back to Josh.

Satchel tossed a "See ya tomorrow" over his shoulder without looking for a response.

He was, however, looking for that waitress who got his attention earlier. He'd have been singing her name in his head already, if only he knew it. Time to fix that.

Once he spied her wiping up a table after the guests had just left, Satchel glided in her direction... Then stopped.

Before she could look up, Janet sensed his presence and playfully warned, "Better make it good..."

Satchel responded with a confident smile but still had to ask, "What do you mean?"

Without looking up, she said, "The silver tongue of black baseball needs four shots before he talks to me. So I'm expecting the poetry that comes next to make Shakespeare quake here."

"Baby girl, if you like poetry..." Satchel began, handing her two tickets, "You're gonna love watching me pitch. Bring your father or one of your little girlfriends to opening day tomorrow. I made sure the seats were nice and close."

Janet pushed the tickets back. "I wish I could, but I'm the new girl, so I got stuck having to work tomorrow."

"Tell Gus I said to let you come," Satchel urged, only half-joking.

"Tell him yourself," Janet countered with a smirk.

Satchel watched Gus and Teddy head toward the back room. "Now may not be the best time for me to make that request... But keep the tickets. And they're along the third base line. I can see the seats from the mound, so if you do come, your beauty can inspire me..."

Janet's smirk widened into a soft smile, and she accepted the tickets. "Thank you kindly."

Satchel put his hat back on to leave. "Now you have a nice night, there. Miss—?"

"My name is Janet," she said, extending her right hand.

Taking her hand and bringing it to his lips for a

quick kiss, Satchel responded, "It sure is."

In the dimly lit back room of his Crawford Grill, Gus took a seat.

Teddy made him a drink from the bar in the corner. Gus sipped, then sought an update from Teddy.

"Well?" Gus prompted, his voice carrying a mixture of anticipation and urgency.

Teddy shook his head, the news not promising. "Asked everyone... No one saw anything. Brick drew a sketch of her, but we need to get it printed. Passed around."

"Anything else?" Gus pressed, his patience thinning.

"No — well... You know I've got a girl in common with Robert from the Courier, right?" Teddy added, shifting the topic slightly.

"I hear things," Gus replied, nodding to acknowledge the small-town nature of their connections.

"She said Robert wanted a secret talk with you. Almost forgot to tell you because I'm focused on the Marie thing," Teddy continued.

"Tell *righteous Robert* every church-going citizen on the Hill will be at the game tomorrow. Give him a ticket in my section, then tell him if he wants a favor from me, he'll have to ask me himself, in public,"

Gus said firmly.

"Okay," Teddy said, ready to relay the message.

Gus continued, "Also, we need to get the card and roulette tables back into this basement. We need the casino running again.That's what we're missing — a little *action* around here, right guys?"

All the suited hoods in the room cheered. The casino was a seasonal income stream for the crew.

"Usual payoffs?" Teddy inquired, knowing the routine well.

"No, build the room first then I'll probably give the cops a complimentary game night before we reopen. Have Teenie take pics of them in the room. That way we threaten to release the photos if anyone loses too much or gains a conscience. Also, it makes the payouts a little cheaper," Gus planned out loud, his strategy clear and calculated.

"Okay," Teddy confirmed.

"And Teddy," Gus called out as Teddy began to leave.

"Yeah?" Teddy turned back to his boss.

"I told this man we'll find his daughter. I want you to turn over every stone you would have turned over if it were Lena. And if you haven't found this girl after that, turn over 20 more stones," Gus commanded.

"Okay," Teddy agreed, his resolve matching that of his boss.

"At this point, I'm not even expecting good news anymore… But I am expecting news," Gus concluded, setting the tone for the continued search.

Having received his orders, Teddy nodded

A knock on the back room door got everyone's immediate attention. Everyone Gus trusted was already in the room. Who could that be?

John walked in, looking concerned. Without a drop of fear even in Gus's presence, he looked right at Teddy.

"What happened to Marie Franks that's got Marion looking scared? And how can I help?"

Chapter 15

Pittsburgh
Saturday, April 30, 1932
7:00am

Of course there had been silent mornings in the Franks household. This was not to be one of them.

Dihanne lay in her daughter's bed, wailing, "Why Marie?! Where is my baby?" between long spells of deep sobs.

Outside, Marion cried silently, but the vibrations from his soul were powerful enough to make the formidable frame of this former boxer shudder.

His hair was completely disheveled.

At some point last night, Marion decided he no longer desired to wear a suit or even a robe, content to exist in his boxers and a stained white sleeveless t-shirt. He'd been deconstructed, demolished even. Internally and externally.

He rocked back and forth in the red rocking chair he had commissioned the second he discovered his wife was pregnant.

He rocked back and forth in the red rocking chair which had raised an entire generation of neighborhood children since she'd grown up.

He rocked back and forth in the red rocking chair his daughter was now old enough to repaint with him, which they did every summer before nursery school began. "A bucket of Red Number 3 from Rusty's Hardware." Little Marie even knew how to order it herself now.

And now he rocked back and forth wondering if he'd ever see his little girl again.

"When I get my hands on whoever did this…"

He continued to rock, until he heard the familiar sound of a bell, the consistent ticking of a bicycle chain, then the thud of a newspaper hitting the porch two doors down. He opened his eyes. Maybe there's news.

Thud.

Another rolled newspaper slammed against a porch like an artillery shell; this time at the house next door.

He was too impatient to continue rocking in the red chair. He stood.

Marion's old boxer reflexes took over when the newspaper was launched in his direction. In a single motion, he caught it with one hand while turning toward the door.

The screen door slammed behind him. Once inside, he walked directly to the kitchen table, already littered with disregarded pages from yesterday's newspapers. Marion and Dihanne had subscriptions to both the Courier and the mainstream Pittsburgh Post-Gazette.

However, when he called the Gazette about reporting his missing daughter, they hung up, as he expected, when he began to describe her to the switchboard operator. He wasn't expecting a follow-up call.

As angry as he was, he couldn't afford to discontinue his subscription out of spite yet. He had to read it in case a "Jane Doe" turned up.

He checked his watch; the Courier would arrive within the hour. Marion opened the Gazette to the Local Happenings section, using every bit of his limited literacy to scan for words which mattered to him: "Black," "girl," or "found." These words were the very definition of *substance of things hoped for*, but alas remained unseen.

Painfully, Dihanne's voice continued the refrain, *"Why Marie?! Where is my baby?!"* Her wails dripped with despair, traveled down the long hallway, and echoed throughout the house.

The phone rang.

Marion sucked in a deep breath before answering.

"This is him. Nothing yet? But you've got a crew of guys combing the streets..."

"Why Marie?! Why MY child?!"

"Oh *that* sound? It's my guilty conscience... Please find my little girl or tell me how I can help. I'll do anything," Marion pleaded before saying, "Thank you for what you're doing Mr. Horne. Teddy!"

Marion hung up and went to the kitchen to fill a glass of water.

He walked down the hallway to Marie's painfully occupied bedroom, carefully pushing the door open.

He set the glass of water on the nightstand next to his wife, then turned his attention to the still-sealed Crampton's Drugs envelope which held her pills.

"Dihanne, you haven't taken any? Baby, the doctor said these pills could help you get some sleep."

Dihanne responded, "Not now, Marion... I can't.

If I take one of them, I'm gonna take all of them."

Chapter 16

Despite the anticipation leading up to this very day, April 30, 1932 arrived in most homes on the Hill with surprising normalcy.

In the Morrison apartment, Mac woke up wearing Josh's baseball cap.

Across town in a modest hotel room, Satchel greeted the day with his usual series of calisthenics: stretches, push-ups, and sit-ups.

Elsewhere, John and Teenie shared a quiet breakfast at a diner, fueling up for the day's coverage, their conversation consisting of small talk.

In the spacious master bedroom at the Greenlee house, Gus awoke in his large bed. He checked the time on the pocket watch resting on his night stand. "Today's the day!"

Janet set her metal hot comb on the same stove eye where her coffee pot had just been moments before.

Her already starched and pressed uniform dress hung from her bedroom door, waiting. Her black heels sat out by the door.

Two tickets to Opening Day at Greenlee Field lay on her breakfast table. What a waste for Satchel to give them to her, albeit a kind gesture.

Acutely aware not to allow a man's words or impulsive kind gestures affect her like a character in a romance novel, Janet couldn't help but think it sweet. Sometimes she liked the sentimental side of herself, other times she hated it. She stared at the tickets, tracing the edges with her fingers.

She stuffed the tickets back into her purse, took two more sips of coffee, then rose to straighten her hair and change into her uniform. She made sure her white gloves were in the bag. As she prepared to walk out the door, it occurred to her... The powder blue sundress she used in emergencies? Janet zipped it into a large garment bag, just in case.

And just in time for Gus's driver to pick her up.

Once she arrived at the back of the club, she pulled out her key and unlocked the door. The driver saw that she made it inside safely, then pulled off to fetch Gus.

Once inside, Janet walked toward the front door to turn on the light above the Crawford Grill sign.

Startled by the sound of snoring, she searched for what *had* to be a bear that had gotten into the club, but instead found Josh Gibson sleeping in a booth on the far side of the bar. He had chosen a booth near a woodburning stove that had gone cold hours ago.

Normally, Janet would be alarmed at such a sight, except this was one of the few things she was told to expect when she was hired.

The ballplayers, especially Josh, knew the Grill as their second home; if they were drunk, they were never kicked out. They were simply told to sleep it off. The alcohol was locked up; they couldn't get into further trouble.

"Doesn't he have a game today?" Janet thought to herself as she looked around for supplies to start the woodburning stove.

The phone rang.

"Hello? Oh, hi...," her voice softened. "Yeah, he's here. Okay... You too! Good luck!"

Janet hung up and walked to the occupied booth.

Gently waking Josh from what had to be an uncomfortable night's sleep, her voice was soft yet firm. "Satchel told me to let you sleep... but remind you to pick a boy."

"A boy?" Josh started, his mind foggy.

"Batboy," Janet clarified with a smile.

"Dammit, so that part wasn't a dream... I really have to hire a kid."

Back at the Morrison home, Mac dressed himself in his freshly washed homemade jersey, which featured the number 20.

He carefully selected oversized "boyish" clothes for his sister Missy, including his normal school baseball cap, then proudly donned his new hat signed by Josh. The two left a note for Michael, which read, "Gone to the game," on the nightstand next to their still-snoring father, before quietly slipping out like cat burglars.

Chapter 17

If there was a stone unturned it was because he didn't know it existed.

The constant refrain of, "What if it were Lena?" kept Edwin "Teddy" Fletcher Horne, Jr. from sleeping.

He was co-owner of the Belmont Hotel on Wylie Avenue and still hadn't seen a bed. He'd only checked back at the front desk to see if there were any updates from the 80 calls around the city looking for the girl.

He talked to Rev. Calvin X. Poole from the Ebenezer Baptist Church, where she could be found most Sundays. Called William Howell at the Kay Boys' Club to see if those boys had seen anything or were curiously missing. Nothing.

Teddy had checked churches and morgues and was still empty handed.

His usually effortless style appeared strained...

He sat in his car shuffling papers, hoping for anything.

Was this a suitor, and things had gone sideways?

Had she eloped?

Was it one of *his* guys?

What he found funny: No one asked him to check with the cops.

What he found not funny: No one asked, because they knew the cops wouldn't have cared.

But Gus cared. Which is why Marion Franks came to him.

And now John cared, which is why he got the sketch replicated by his friends at the Courier off the books and free of charge. He'd even snuck a tiny missing persons report at the bottom of the front page. It was only a few lines with a phone number, but John had killed himself to get it done right after his quick meeting with Gus.

What if it were Lena? What if there was someone out there and Lena was next?

He needed answers. And he needed them quickly.

This was deeper than his intention to never let Gus down.

He could very well have been the last person to see

her.

His heart sank.

Eyes blurred with tears, Teddy thought it best to close them and try to relax for a minute.

Jolted by a tap on his window, Teddy snapped to attention. The sun was up, and his crew found him sleeping in his car. In a hurry, he fixed his hair, grabbed his hat, and got out of the car.

"You guys find anything?"

"No sir. We were coming to check with you in case you had any updates."

Teddy, visibly frustrated, made it a point to remain calm with the young men who reported to him.

He smoothed over his hair, steadied his voice, and repeated, "Get me whatever you can find." This time adding, " And offer a reward."

The crew looked at one another.

"I've got 300 dollars for a tip that leads to finding this girl and I got 300 dollars for the man who brings me the tip."

Chapter 18

Greenlee Field. The morning buzzed with activity as Satchel Paige pulled up in his Cadillac convertible alongside the Black Yankees' bus.

Gus arrived shortly after with architect Louis Bellinger, and together they showed the press and visiting team around the newly completed facilities.

Inside Greenlee Field, the Pittsburgh Crawfords suited up, then headed out to the field for warm-ups and batting practice. Mac, wearing his hat and jersey, was among the early arrivals, sister Missy in tow. He looked around the bustling stadium and turned to Missy with a plan.

"We don't have tickets yet, but I'm gonna see if I can get us in somehow. I need you to stay with me, alright? When I move you move, got it?" He tried to sound confident for both their sakes.

"Alright," Missy replied, then paused thoughtfully. "I just thought of something."

"What?"

"You always practice hitting and catching... And throwing... You even run well."

"Well as far as I know, that's how baseball is played," Mac responded, a slight smile crossing his face.

"But you're bad at talking trash to the other players," Missy pointed out innocently.

"No one keeps score based on what's said," Mac replied, trying to dismiss her concern.

"Yeah, but all the other kids are good at it... And then you make mistakes," she observed, causing Mac to laugh. However, his laughter quickly turned to a frown as he failed to find the flaw in humoring his kid sister.

"You got anything good for me?" Mac asked, half-joking.

"Not yet, but if... When we get inside... I'll be listening just in case. I even brought my notepad," Missy said, ready to help her big brother in any way she could.

"Okay, well put that away for now, Missy." Mac, still looking for an opening in security, hurried his sister toward the taxi stand, searching for adults to trail behind.

Of all the game day rituals Josh Gibson adopted in his baseball career, none included finding a batboy. He felt kind of weird about the guys who volunteered for such tasks. But with the ball team being more than just a uniform and all, he found himself considering what qualities would make a good one.

That kid should be well behaved but not too sensitive, there WILL be a lot of smoking and dugout talk. Can't have a kid who couldn't handle the environment. That would be cruel.

Then again they have an important job to do. They gotta be responsible, but not take themselves too seriously.

Josh wondered if he had to interview the kids like it was his first job at Gimbels Department store. Should he interview the parents first?

Then something caught his eye.

A brand new Crawfords hat hovered through the crowd, but too close to the ground to be a player.

Today is opening day, so it's the first time the general public has ever seen this hat. And even if they'd seen it before, it was impossible for the average person to buy one.

Josh found himself more curious about this mystery hat than his recruiting responsibilities. His eyes widened. Oh! Mystery solved.

Josh hurriedly tapped the driver on the shoulder and

told him to slow down.

Rolling down the window, Josh called out, "Hey kid!"

Mac and Missy continued to walk. Josh called out again, more specifically this time, "It's McGray, but your friends call you Mac, right?"

Mac stopped, confused, skeptical even. He gripped Missy's hand tightly. Here he was trying to avoid being seen and then gets called by his full *official* name.

Josh stepped out of the car.

"Hurry up now, I gotta give you these tickets so I can get back to work."

The children walked toward the car.

Mac's confusion quickly turned to disbelief once he recognized who was calling him.

"You know my whole name?" Mac asked, astonished.

"Yeah, just like I know your dad's name is Mike?" Josh continued, piecing things together for him.

"Yeah..." Mac responded, still in shock.

"Where is he?" Josh inquired, genuinely interested.

"He's resting..." Mac explained.

Josh, who held three tickets in his hand, took back one of them and said, "Good... Take these two tickets... They should be nice and close."

Josh turned around to get back in the cab when it hit him...

"Hey Mac..."

The kids turn around,again.

"If I can promise you can keep an eye on your sister from those seats, do you want a job? It pays 50 cents..."

Chapter 19

Inside the Crawford Grill, Janet busied herself by cleaning the bar, her ears tuned to the radio that was broadcasting the game live. The bar was unusually quiet for a game day, the absence of the usual crowd making the space feel larger than usual.

As the melody of the national anthem flowed from the speaker, Bobby Davis and Jeff Lee walked into the bar. The anthem echoed through the nearly empty room as they looked around, puzzled by the silence.

"We heard this was a jumping spot…" Jeff remarked, scanning the deserted bar.

"Yeah, where is everyone?" Bobby asked, his voice carrying a hint of disappointment.

At Greenlee Field, the atmosphere was charged with excitement. Gus, dressed in a striking white suit, sat atop a red Packard convertible parked in center field.

Subtle.

As the final notes of the national anthem faded into a round of applause and cheers, the focus shifted to the field. Missy was perched on a small chair next to the dugout, her eyes wide with excitement and a bit of awe at the scene unfolding before her. Next to her, decked out in a batboy uniform, Mac looked every part an official member of the Pittsburgh Crawfords.The umpire stepped forward, his voice cutting through the buzz of the crowd with the words everyone was waiting for...

"Play ball!"

Chapter 20

3rd inning
BLACK YANKEES: 0
CRAWFORDS: 0
2 outs

The Hill District showed up excited and loud. Opening day at Greenlee Field was probably as much a social event as it was mass at the newest cathedral for negro league baseball.

The sound of a fastball smacking the palm of a well-worn leather glove resonated sharply.

"Strike one!" the umpire called out, his voice firm over the noise.

Satchel, ever the showman on the mound, chuckled and called out to the batter, "Now that was about as slow as I could have thrown that one for ya."

Unamused, the batter grunted.

"Now this time, it's gonna curve a little to the left, but don't worry it'll end up right over the plate," Satchel chided, setting up his next pitch with the confidence of a seasoned player. He pitched again; the glove's pop sounded like a gunshot, the batter swung and missed.

"Strike two!"

The batter was clearly frustrated.

Not missing a beat, Satchel pointed to Mr. Bojangles behind home plate and said, "Now, for my next number!" He mimicked tap dancing moves, which drew laughter from some, and head-shakes from others.

"Can you just shut the hell up and pitch?" the batter snapped.

"I think it's physically impossible for him," the catcher chimed in, amused by the exchange.

"I'm trynna help YOU out. Now granted, it doesn't seem to be doing you that much good, so I'll shut up and pitch. Good luck," Satchel replied, ending the banter.

"Thanks!" the batter said, hoping to regain his focus.

Then came the sudden pop of the glove again. "Strike three!""Shit.... I didn't even see that one, and I threw it!" Satchel exclaimed, surprised by his own pitch as he walked toward the dugout with the rest of the team, ready for the bottom of the inning.

"Hey guys, don't let ol' Hubbard up there scare ya. Don't tell nobody. But I *heard* when he was born he almost starved to death?"

"Why's that Satch?" Josh asked, playing along.

"His ma got confused and had been nursing the dog... Seems she couldn't tell the difference," Satchel delivered the punchline, causing a ripple of laughter through the dugout.

Mac laughed so hard he almost choked. He shot a quick look at Missy, who laughed and nodded, waving her pencil.

"Already wrote it down," she said, having captured the humor and camaraderie of the moment.

Chapter 21

4th Inning (top)
BLACK YANKEES: 0
CRAWFORDS: 0
2 outs

It was truly a first at the Crawford Grill. Janet was bored.

She tried to look busy. She'd cleaned everything. She hovered around the hostess stand, stealing occasional glances at her only two customers, Jeff and Bobby, who were still working on their first round of drinks.

Of course Janet knew everyone drank at their own pace, but these two men drank cold beer slower than she'd seen other people enjoy warm whiskey; slower than grass has been known to grow.

They'd talk, then they'd look at her, then they'd go back to talking.

Janet had only seen such slow drinking from customers who eventually had trouble paying their tabs. She felt she may need back-up. But everyone was at the game. Well, almost everyone.

She approached the phone behind the bar; next to it was a list of numbers in case of emergency. Quickly, she located Brick's name and dialed the number. A woman answered.

Janet introduced herself as Janet the waitress on duty at the Grill looking for Brick because of a security concern.

The woman said, "Hold on."

In the background, Janet heard her call "LAMAR! Some girl at Gus's spot needs you."

Brick picked up the phone.

"Hello?"

"Brick, it's Janet. I've got two guys here at the bar that I can't tell if they're cops or broke, but their sips are slow, smaller than a sparrow's, and they're being weird."

"I was on my way to the game. But I'll head over there first. Make sure everything is okay."

"Thanks."

Janet hung up the phone and sighed.

7th inning (middle)
BLACK YANKEES:0
CRAWFORDS:0

During the seventh inning stretch, Mr. Bojangles performed a tap dance on top of the visiting team's dugout, much to the crowd's delight.

Gus watched from his seat, pleased with the reaction, but preoccupied with other concerns.

Meanwhile, Robert approached Gus's section with his wife and Cumberland Posey, likely to discuss matters of mutual interest.

Back in the press box, Teenie and John endured the game's slow pace.

"Pitchers' duels are so boooooooring," Teenie complained, alternating his focus between binoculars and a camera. John, who was typing, paused and agreed with a simple "Yeah..."

Teenie, ever curious, asked, "You know what you're gonna write about?"

"Nope. What are you looking at?" John replied, genuinely interested.

"Nothing and yet everything at the same time," Teenie mused. "Say... What do you suppose Robert is saying to Gus right now?"

"Huh?"

"I mean our boss just walked in with Cumberland Posey."

John's interest piqued, he lunged toward Teenie, "Let me see that!" Snatching the binoculars from Teenie, he was eager to catch a glimpse.

Smitty, the teenage pitcher with the directionless fastball, was at the game like everyone else. Sitting in the stands eating a vanilla ice cream cone, he noticed the Crawford's batboy looked familiar.

No. It couldn't be... It's that kid Mac from yesterday? And he's wearing an actual *uniform?*

He'd have traded a 1000 ice cream cones to switch places with Mac in that moment. I mean when you think about it, who really *needs* ice cream anyway?.

Back at Crawford Grill, Jeff and Bobby moved to the bar and struck up a conversation with Janet. "So you're saying a colored man named Gus, what's his name?" Jeff asked.

"Greenlee," Janet filled in.

"Built and owns that new stadium?" Bobby added, a note of disbelief in his voice.

"Yeah," Janet confirmed.

"During this depression?" Jeff was incredulous.

"That's what I'm saying…" Janet replied, her tone indicating that she too found the accomplishment remarkable.

"How 'bout that, Bobby?" Jeff turned to his friend.

"Where did he get his steel from?" Bobby asked.

"I have no idea where they got the steel," Janet admitted, then walked away from the bar back to the hostess stand where the radio was. She unplugged it.

Left alone, Jeff and Bobby shared a moment of contemplation. "There are good men trying to figure out how to feed their families, and this nigger is building *stadiums*?" Jeff remarked bitterly.

Bobby replied,"I know. If it weren't for the surprise cash the other night, I might have had to pack up the family and move back down south."

Janet returned with the radio and plugged it in behind the bar.

"Now where do you suppose he got the money to do all that?" Bobby pondered.

"Well look around, you're sitting in his bar," she pointed out, a hint of pride in her voice.

"Huh?" Bobby was taken aback.

"Goddammit... he's a bootlegger," Jeff concluded, his tone a mix of awe and resentment.

Seeing an opportunity to redirect the conversation, Janet said, "So I'm guessing you all want to leave. Now."

"Nah... Our usual spot got roughed up when a bunch of us steelworkers got laid off," Jeff began.

"We're looking for a new spot and this looks right nice... Go 'head and pour us two more beers, will ya. Shit, we're here now," Bobby decided, settling into the unexpected sanctuary of the Crawford Grill.

"Coming right up," Janet replied, all the while wondering, "Where the hell is Brick?"

Chapter 22

Bottom of the 8th (bottom)
BLACK YANKEES: 0
CRAWFORDS: 0
1 out

Disinterested in the scoreboard, Satchel Paige fixated on two empty seats in the stands, along the third base line. The look on his face hinted at personal stakes beyond the game's outcome.

Meanwhile, Josh approached Mac, who was taking practice swings. Observing Mac's form, Josh commented, arms crossed, "You look like you know what you're doing with that."

"My dad throws me balls at the sandlot...," Mac

responded, focusing on his swings while keeping a watchful eye on the game.

Josh nodded, connecting the dots. "On Sundays... He said something 'bout that. Can you hit? Like really hit?"

"All day every day, except when it counts," Mac admitted.

"Strike three!" The umpire yelled as third baseman Jud Wilson struck out.

"Hold that thought...," Mac said, pausing the conversation.

Josh shook his head and smiled, impressed by how seriously Mac took his job.

Chapter 23

Brick entered through the back door, eyes so busy looking for the potential trouble that he missed Janet's obvious relief.

He spotted Bobby and Jeff by the bar. They were definitely drunk, but he wanted to gauge just how much.

"Good afternoon, gentlemen. You guys having fun?"

Bobby looked up then back to his drink, resolute in his decision not to speak.

Brick, familiar with this brand of disrespect, knew the type, but with higher priorities occupying his mental space, he let it go. After all, it *was* 1932.

Turning his back to them, Brick reached into his pocket to pull out the sketch of Marie's face, which had been printed by the Courier staff. He tucked this into the top left corner behind the bar, so that it was in full view of these two miscreants. Without a word, he opened the door to the back office.

Bobby, squinting at the picture, couldn't help himself. "You think that's…"

"Of course it's her. But it ain't no use in them calling the police, and if they did it ain't like they gon' think to look up at ol' Myer's pond, nobody goes up there," Jeff said with a cynical laugh.

"You think she's still alive?"

"It's not like I'm going up there to check. I mean… We had our fun. She's tied up. I'll go back up there in a week or so, after I'm sure she's dead, and then I'm gon' burn her with the rest of the trash. It'll be simple enough."

"Between the layoff and Sue not letting me near her since that kid was born, I was angry but maybe we shouldn't have…," Bobby's voice trailed off, thoughts clouded by regret.

"No sense getting a weak stomach now. Calm down… I mean… There's nothing to worry about?" Jeff tried to reassure him.

Janet exited the ladies' room and was about to turn the corner into the main room when she overheard the tail end of their conversation. Realizing she probably shouldn't have heard it, she quickly stepped back toward the ladies' room and loudly closed the door, drawing the men's attention. Both turned to see her turn the corner toward the bar.

Bobby's gaze dropped to his drink while Jeff kept a skeptical eye on Janet.

She averted her eyes, but once behind the bar, she looked up at them with a forced casual smile, hands trembling beneath the bar top.

"You two like whiskey?" she asked, masking her anxiety.

"Yes! I! DO!" Bobby exclaimed eagerly, desperate for another distraction.

"Who doesn't?" Jeff responded, watching Janet closely for any sign that she was onto them.

"Well, since y'all are new to the bar... And we'd like to make y'all regulars, I'm allowed to give y'all each a free shot," she offered, maintaining a facade of hospitality.

"How about that, Jeff... Looks like it's our lucky day!" Bobby slurred.

"Yeah... How 'bout that," Jeff agreed, tone somber, mind racing.

Janet turned and reached for a bottle on the top shelf. In the mirror behind the bar, she noticed the sketch of Marie, as well asJeff's watchful eyes.

She turned around, facing them.

"This is the boss's favorite, and it's fresh off the boat from Ireland," she announced, trying to sound upbeat.

"Alright, pour it up," Bobby urged, ready for the drink.

"Go ahead and pour it already," Jeff demanded.

Janet grabbed two shot glasses, then hesitated, looking around the nearly empty bar. Jeff's fists clenched in anticipation, ready to act if needed. Recognizing the tension, Janet decided to be more generous.

"Since nobody's here... Let's say we make it a double for each of you," she suggested, trading the shot glasses for rocks glasses. She filled each one, emptying the bottle.

Jeff's hands relaxed while she poured.

"Cheers!!" Bobby toasted, lifting his glass.

"Yeah... Cheers," Jeff echoed, his voice still carrying a hint of unease but relieved by the drink.

"Oh come on, man... Why aren't you smiling? C'mon, free Irish whiskey!" Bobby tried to lighten the mood, words slurring.

"Your friend has a point. In fact, since I'm not going to make it to the game and it looks like I'm gonna be stuck here with y'all... Let me go to the stockroom, grab another bottle, and I may have one myself."

"Now you're talking," Bobby responded enthusiastically.

Jeff, now at ease, happily sipped his drink. Janet tossed the empty bottle in the trash and walked to the back.

Softly, she tapped on the office door. When Brick opened it, Janet locked eyes with him.

"I don't know where Marie is, but those two inside... They do," she whispered urgently.

"How do you know?" Brick questioned, brow furrowed."Liquored tongues are looser than most, and they don't whisper as quietly as they think they do..." Janet replied, her voice low and ominous.

Brick sprung into action.

"Go out the back... Lock the door, and get Teddy... He should be outside the stadium waiting for news. Tell him to bring his keys. Don't worry, I'll keep 'em here, 'till Teddy arrives." Janet slipped out the back and locked the door. Brick walked past Jeff and Bobby to lock the front door. He spun the sign around to indicate, "Sorry, we're closed."

Teddy leaned against his car, which he'd parked on the sidewalk in front of the stadium, not a sanctioned spot of any kind. He knew no one would tell him to move. A half-finished hand-rolled cigarette between his fingers, Teddy was flanked by three men in fedoras. Suddenly, he spotted Janet running toward him, and straightened up to receive her.

He held up his hands. "Slow down, little lady... What's the rush?"

Janet bent over, hands on her knees, trying to catch

her breath. "These two guys..."

Teddy frowned. "Take your time, wha?"

Janet swallowed, forcing the words out. "Marie..."

That was all it took. Teddy's entire demeanor shifted. His face hardened, and he flicked his fingers, launching what was left of his cigarette to parts unknown.

"Brick has them at the Grill," Janet continued, her voice steady now.

Teddy locked eyes with her. "You sure?"

Janet nodded once, gaze unshaken. That was enough.

Teddy's expression darkened. He turned slightly, signaling the men at his side. "Get in, let's go." He started the car and carefully pulled onto the street, turning right.

One of the men pointed down the street. "Boss, the Grill is the other way..."

Teddy, without taking his eyes from the road, said, "We have to make a stop first."

Janet exhaled, steeling herself. She straightened her skirt, smoothed her hair, then turned and approached the security guard at the entrance of the stadium.

"Hey Janet!" the guard smiled.

She reached into her bag, still catching her breath. "I've got a ticket here somewhere..."

The guard waved her off. "Don't even worry about that. They're just starting the ninth inning... Plus, it's you. Gus's people get in free."

The sharp crack of a bat echoed from inside, followed by an eruption of cheers.

Janet didn't waste another second. She hurried through the gate and disappeared into the crowd.

Chapter 24

9th Inning (top)
BLACK YANKEES: 0
CRAWFORDS: 0
1 out

The game teetered on the edge of a sharp knife. Suddenly, skillfully, a Black Yankees batter cracked a single and got on base. Satchel Paige leaned forward, readying for his next pitch, when the runner took a chance and stole second. Challenged, Satchel was too focused to engage in his signature banter.

Meanwhile, at the Frank House, Teddy's car disrupted the quiet afternoon. Marion, who had been sitting on the front porch in a sleeveless t-shirt, caught Teddy's eye once the car rolled to a stop.

Without words or thought, Marion ran into his house, slid on a pair of pants, boots, then a jacket, forgoing a button-up shirt.

He quickly combed his hair, kissed his wife, then grabbed his hat before heading out the door.

Once Marion was inside the car, he and Teddy sped off from the curb, the urgency of their mission unspoken.

The radio announcer's voice broke through, "That sacrifice fly is deep to right-center field... It looks like the runner on second will score!"

BLACK YANKEES: 1
CRAWFORDS: 0
2 outs

Satchel's shoulders slumped while he took extra time around the mound. No jokes this time.

Now inside the stadium, Janet approached Gus and whispered something into his ear. Gus's subtle movements informed his entourage it was time to go.

He offered Janet his seat as stood up, but she pointed

toward the third base line instead. Shrugging, Gus shook hands with Cumberland Posey and Robert Vann before taking off.

Janet continued down the third base line, and took her seat just as Satchel prepared to pitch again. The frustration of his blown shutout was evident on his face.

With white-gloved hands, Janet stood to offer him a sharp military salute. He saw this, and something within him was set aflame.

Satchel straightened up, switching from defeat to determination. With renewed vigor, he declared, "Ya'll done fucked up and made me mad now. Just for that, no one is gonna see another pitch. That's my word."

His wind-up was fluid, aim locked, but when the pitch found the catcher's glove, it popped loudly.

"Strike one!," the umpire called. Another wind-up, another throw, another pop. "Strike two!"

Final pitch. Satchel's intensity was clear. He delivered a blistering fastball. The batter could only flail, helpless.

"Strike three!"   And the batter walked away, defeated.

Feeling the crowd's energy, Satchel returned a salute to Janet, who clapped along with fans rising for a standing ovation. The shift in momentum was palpable.

Chapter 25

Gus and his entourage of fedora-wearing suits filed into Crawford Grill, passing a "We're Open" sign. A crew member served as the on-duty bartender..

They moved through the main dining room, past the back room, and down the stairs to a hidden basement door. Inside, poker and roulette tables were stacked against the walls.

In this shadowy basement, Jeff and Bobby were suspended by their wrists, faces bloodied and bruised. Nearby, Marion's hands were submerged in a bucket of ice.

Gus, removing his jacket and settling into a chair, lit a cigar with pretentious flair. His calm demeanor contrasted sharply with the tension in the room.

Jeff began, defiantly, "You got no idea how badly

y'all messed up... As soon as we get out of here—"

Gus interrupted with a chuckle, prompting Bobby to ask, "Wh-what's so funny?"

"You two thinking you're going to get out of here."

While Gus spoke, Marion removed his hand from the ice, gripped a roll of quarters, and struck Jeff in the face. Hard.

Gus continued, "And then I have a police department that wouldn't investigate y'all if I dropped you off on their doorstep like unwanted twin orphans in front of Our Lady of who gives a fuck."

After hitting Bobby, Marion returned his hand to the ice, face contorted with pain and resolve.

"My baseball team — that I paid entirely too much for — looks like they're going to lose their first game in my new stadium. I'm gonna need myself a win today, and it looks like it's gonna be you two." He took a long pull on his cigar, smoke curling in the dim light.

Gus and Teddy left the basement. Marion wound up. And let loose.

Chapter 26

9th **Inning (bottom)**
BLACK YANKEES: 0
CRAWFORDS: 0
1 out

Mac knelt with a bat, next to Josh and the rest of the Crawfords.

"Looks like you're coming up in the bottom of the ninth," he remarked, trying to make conversation amid the tension.

"Looks like it," Josh replied, his tone resigned, yet focused.

"Nervous?" Mac asked, glancing sideways at Josh.

"Yeah," Josh admitted.

"Because of the crowd?"

"Yeah. Got any advice?" Genuinely, Josh turned to Mac.

Mac's gaze dropped to the concrete, a sense of shame washing over him. "Sir, I wish... When I was in this position... I flied out to center field."

"Yeah... Heard about that," Josh said with a hint of empathy.

"From who?" Mac looked up abruptly, surprised.

"One of your fans," Josh revealed.

Just then, the manager's voice echoed from across the dugout. "GIBSON! You're on deck!"

Mac handed Josh his bat.

But as Josh walked toward the on-deck circle, Mac, processing Josh's words, called out, "Wait! I have fans?"

"Of course you do," Josh assured, stopping to face Mac directly before heading into one of the most critical moments of the game. He paused, then added with a grin, "Hell, *I'm* one of 'em."

Mac's jaw fell open.

Chapter 27

"Whose idea was it to go get Marion?" Gus asked, seated back upstairs at the main bar.

Without hesitation, Teddy replied, "Mine."

"Why?" Gus probed further.

"'Cause if it was my Lena? I'd kill whoever bruised their knuckles in place of mine..." Gus nodded, satisfied with the answer. He appreciated loyalty and the raw honesty behind the motivation. Then, looking back at Teddy, he continued, "And..."

Both men spoke in unison, a moment of camaraderie evident in their tone, "He was the local heavyweight champ from 1924 to 1927."

Gus smiled. "Smart. Oh, you know, Robert Vann came to the seats?"

"Weeks of babysitting his errand boy paid off?" Teddy guessed, raising an eyebrow.

"Sometimes the long play works best, he even showed up with Posey," Gus remarked, a hint of pride in his voice.

"What'd they want?" Teddy leaned in, curious about the new development.

"For me to back that Roosevelt fella the Dems are putting up," Gus disclosed, swirling his drink.

"You're not in a position to donate to a campaign—" Teddy started.

"Hell, I couldn't even get the lights done because I dropped a mint on that lineup."

Teddy smiled, seeing Gus's strategic play. "So you got him to bet on the game... What's the bet?"

"The next game. We win, he sponsors the lights... With a Pittsburgh Courier logo on the scoreboard."

"And if you don't?" Teddy pressed, recognizing the stakes.

"Then he pays for the lights in secret and I back his candidate."

"But you were—," Teddy began, but Gus interrupted.

"I know I was thinking of backing the Roosevelt kid anyway. DuBois likes him, and he ain't wrong most times. But if they don't offer me something, I'll look like a turncoat to the Republicans... If given a choice, it's always better to look like a mercenary than indecisive," Gus concluded, strategy laid bare.

"Hmph... Nice play," Teddy acknowledged.

A wry smile crossing his features, Gus said, "I've been in politics way longer than they have." Just then, the basement door burst open. Brick shouted, "A shed on the south side of Myer's pond behind the steel mill!"

"Alright, that's where we're going. Take those boys out the back. And put 'em in the trunk of your car..."

Brick nodded and turned back to give everyone else the orders.

Gus wasn't done, "And Brick?"

"Yeah, boss?"

"Is she alive?"

"They don't know."

"Get some blankets just in case."

Chapter 28

9ᵗʰ Inning (bottom)
BLACK YANKEES: 0
CRAWFORDS: 0
2 outs

Hope and anxiety hanging heavily in the evening air, the crowd's energy was nearly tangible. Josh, determined and focused, approached the batter's box, taking a few practice swings. During the at-bat he fouled off several pitches.

While Josh was getting ready for the next pitch, George Scales,manager of the Black Yankees, called, "Timeout," then walked to the mound to talk to the pitcher.

During the brief timeout, Josh noted the entire Crawfords team was staring at him. In fact, every eye in this new baseball stadium was staring at him. Then he saw Mac's face. Responsible, mature and yet still very much a child.

Josh decided what to do next while watching Scales walk back to the Black Yankees dugout.

The umpire called, "Resume play!"

When the pitcher began his motion, Josh adjusted his stance slightly, shifting his left foot *inward* by a couple inches.

Satchel, watching from the dugout, muttered to himself, "You make your own luck, huh?" While the pitcher wound up, he strolled toward the stands near the third base line, moving closer to where Janet was seatedThe pitch was thrown, and Josh hit the ball high and deep into center field. The entire crowd rose to its feet, a wave of hopeful fans watching as the ball arced through the sky. Satchel, however, seemed more focused on reaching Janet than watching the end of the play. He already knew what was going to happen.

The center fielder caught the ball. The game was over, and the Crawfords lost.

Once at Janet's side, Satchel broke the silence which had fallen over the crowd. "So... You made it?"

"I did."

"Got plans for dinner?" he ventured.

"Not yet," she smiled.

"Let me..." Satchel paused, grinning as he glanced at the dugout, remembering where he was. "...Get showered and changed inside, and I'll see what I can do about that."

"Okay, Mr. Paige," she smiled, her eyes flickered.

Chapter 29

Teenie entered the press box with two beers in hand, breaking the tension with this small victory. "So. They lost, but I scored us a couple of cold ones."

"Yeah? Nice...," John responded, focused on his typewriter.

"How's the column coming?" Teenie asked.

Rubbing his chin thoughtfully, John said, "Well, it's coming."

"Any poetry?" Teenie settled into his seat.

John hesitated, typed a few more words then, "A few random thoughts... But how about...," as he began to read aloud:

"Sure the Pittsburgh Crawfords' expensive new roster

At Meyer's Pond, behind the steel mill, at gunpoint, Jeff and Bobby were forced to open a windowless shed. Inside that shed, in her shredded uniform dress, was an unconscious Marie. Her hands and feet were knotted to a hitching post; her pulse was faint but present.

Both men were stripped down to nothing and shot. Made to look as though the two men had been killed when discovered during a tryst.

"The things we did in the shadows."

Teddy's car pulled up in front of the Frank house. Dihanne waited on the porch.

Marion Frank exited the passenger side of the car. He opened the rear door, motioning for her to get in. Dihanne ran to meet him, tears streaming. She saw his bloodied knuckles and kissed his hands before crumbling into his arms.

"The things we did selfishly for ourselves."

Marie breathing, but still unconscious as she laid on

a bed at the back of a modest infirmary with a gentle nurse attending to her.

Feeling helpless, Dihanne witnessed this nurse care for her daughter in ways she could not. Her baby. Marie. Dihanne was no longer in the dark. Nor was Marie. The family would face whatever came next, together.

After a few hours, Brick visited with a garment bag he'd picked up from Sam Reznik & Sons. No one would open it for months, but if they had, they would have the lemon yellow dress.

"Or the sacrifices we've made for others."

Gus Greenlee adjusted his tie before stepping in front of a pool of black photographers at a ribbon-cutting ceremony, smiling and waving a printed Roosevelt campaign flyer. Robert Vann nodded in approval at the side.

"No matter whether we've won or lost on that day...
The most important thing we can do is... Prepare."

At the sandlot, cane in hand, Michael joined his kids and Josh Gibson. Mac wore his Crawford bat boy jersey, and Missy wore her big brother's hand-painted jersey and Josh's paint-stained hat.

Michael approached the mound, holding a bag of baseballs. Josh knelt behind Mac to catch and coach him.

"Because the challenges will come again. They always do."

Missy sat behind the backstop, hurling playful insults while Mac practiced. Whatever she said made everyone laugh, but Mac focused, gripped the bat tighter, and widened his stance with his left leg, careful to add only two more inches.

The pitch.

Mac swings…

"There will always be another game."

And echoing throughout the sandlot, the unmistakable crack of a baseball hit by a bat rang loud and clear.

"There's always tomorrow."

Acknowledgements

FWF for the flashlight
SLG for your red pen
&
BRB for the bow...